METHUEN PAIRED READING STORYBOOKS

Candy's Camel

Bill Gillham

Illustrated by Margaret Chamberlain

Methuen Children's Books

Some people have cats.

Some people have dogs.

But Candy had a camel.

Only Candy could see it.

"Mind my camel!" Candy said.

The camel slept by her bed.

It sat up to the table.

It even came in the bath
with her.

Candy loved her camel.

But one day she lost it.

Candy looked everywhere . . .

In the toy cupboard . . .

In the toilet . . .

Under the stairs . . .

Behind the garden shed . . . .

Candy cried and went
to bed all alone.

But in the morning
Camel was there again.

And there was something
lumpy in Candy's bed.

"Don't squash my baby!"
said Camel.

Candy carried the baby
downstairs.

And they all sat down
to breakfast together.

There just wasn't room
for anyone else!

How to pair read

1 Sit the child next to you, so that you can both see the book.

2 Tell the child you are *both* going to read the story *at the same time*. To begin with the child will be hesitant: adjust your speed so that you are reading almost simultaneously, *pointing to the words* as you go.

3 If the child makes a mistake, repeat the correct word but *keep going* so that fluency is maintained.

4 Gradually increase your speed once you and the child are reading together.

5 As the child becomes more confident, lower your voice and, progressively, try dropping out altogether.

6 If the child stumbles or gets stuck, give the correct word and continue 'pair-reading' to support fluency, dropping out again quite quickly.

7 Read the story *right through* once a day but not more than twice, so that it stays fresh.

8 After about 5–8 readings the child will usually be reading the book independently.

In its original form paired reading was first described by RTT Morgan and E Lyon (1979), in a paper published in the Journal of Child Psychology and Psychiatry.